JUST A TICK OF WHIMSY

VOLUME 2

B. A. PAUL

CONTENTS

FOREWORD

Stuff… We all have it. Stuff we don't need. Stuff we don't want. Stuff
we can't live without. Stuff to put stuff in…

In the last few years, we've cleaned out three estates of family
members that have passed or needed to downsize.

And oh, my, the stuff.

After each clean-out, I went home exhausted and started tossing
and donating *my* stuff. Thinking, if I die or become otherwise inca-
pacitated, I surely don't want my kids to deal with it.

Then it begins:

Except that ugly yellow turtle cookie jar that was my grandfather's
because it reminds me of his stories of hunting for snapping turtles
along muddy riverbanks and I can still see where it lived in my grand-
parents' house.

Speaking of them, my grandmother found flower-shaped quartz
rocks from Lake Pleasant in Arizona decades ago, so don't touch
those. Or any aunt- or grandmother-made quilt. Ever. Never ever
touch the quilts.

Speaking of aunts, leave those two hardback copies of *Where's
Waldo* alone. I say I'm keeping them because they're tall enough to

support a broken shelf on my bookcase, but really, it's *Waldo*, and my aunt gave them to me.

And speaking of gifts, my husband gave me a dog for my birthday ten years ago. Leave his red collar hanging on my rearview mirror, please. May the pup rest in peace.

Speaking of death, my pink marble egg that fits so nicely in the palm of my hand and is so cool and heavy, and my dad gave it to me one Easter—may he rest in peace. It was the same Easter that the sparrow flew into the house and our Boston Terriers went berserk and oh, the chaos...

And speaking of feathered things, leave my birds alone. The vintage tropical bird figurines that I really did buy at a yard sale to flip on eBay but they ended up with their own special shelf in my sunroom. And the seller was an eccentric old woman who'd collected tropical bird figurines her entire life and insisted on giving me a tour of *her* sunroom where hundreds of birds covered the walls and tables...

And as I toss and donate, I remember things that I *don't* have any longer. The corsages from prom, my wedding bouquet and a unicorn autograph book—all destroyed in a basement flood.

And speaking of unicorns, my entire unicorn collection that I sold at a garage sale when I was getting married and it was time to grow up and save space for apartment life. Hundreds of unicorn figurines amassed over my childhood. Each one magical to me at one time or another.

You get the picture. We assign memories to objects. The items aren't needed and wouldn't mean diddly squat to anyone else, but we gain comfort with them.

Some objects mark victories or terrible heartache. Think of the relics stored in museums behind glass cases, under lock and key. Permanent banners of victories, accomplishments, and innovation. And around the corner, in another wing, memorials of war, death, and destruction.

Think of your own banners and memorials. Your first-place

trophy versus the consolation ribbon. The wedding band you wear every day. Or the one rattling around in your junk drawer.

Triumph and defeat seem to be etched into the object's "memory." A permanent echo of the past— and only a glimpse of the object is enough to bring smiles or reopen wounds.

Fiction writing gives authors the ultimate platform to play with an object's emotional and "what if" power. Think Hemingway's six-word novel: *For sale: baby shoes, never worn.* Think of Tolkien's ring sheltering its wearer in invisibility while heightening the senses. Think of Baum's shoes and Lewis's wardrobe transporting characters to magical worlds. Think of Lucas's whip in the hands of Indiana Jones, or his glowing light saber in the hands of Luke Skywalker fighting evil in a galaxy far, far away.

But none of the objects mean anything without the characters behind them. We love Frodo, Indiana, and Dorothy. We love our mothers and dads and aunts and the occasional eccentric old bird-collector. Without the character, the connection is lost and the object really is diddly squat—just another trinket collecting dust.

I love the what-ifs of objects, especially old rusty and moth-eaten ones. What has that old camera seen? What about the globe that isn't quite round anymore? That golden cat statue guarding the flower bed —is it marking the passing of a beloved pet? Or is it stolen, a token of some long-deserved revenge? The object sparks the wonder. The characters bring it to life…

Take a look around your home. Clean out the junk drawer or the top of the hall closet. When an object causes you to pause, hold it for a moment. Smell it. Examine it. Then close your eyes.

And remember.

Happy reading!

B. A. Paul

QUILLS

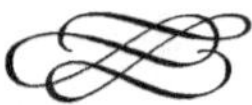

Darling's father committed a crime that sent her into servitude under the Master Scribe. She spends her days collecting feather quills and blending inks for the Scribe's magical writings, all the while unsure of her mother's welfare and of her own future. But when the Scribe's magic falters, Darling sees a way out...

*D*arling sprang from the feather bed and darted to the window, her bare feet expertly avoiding the stray nail heads that had worked their way loose from the planked floor. The noonday sun beat on the dingy pane that she'd not cared to clean in months. Why bother? She was well acquainted with the expansive barnyard below, and that's one reason she'd retreated to the upstairs loft for a siesta after her morning chores. Just for a bit. While he was busy.

To escape the cacophony of quacking and squawking and chirps.

To escape the constant picking and plucking and egg-grabbing required to maintain Apprentice Scribe's property.

To escape Apprentice's incessant barking of orders so particular that no servant, maid, or hired hand could ever follow to his liking.

The ruckus that'd drawn her from her nap was not of feathered fowls—she was accustomed to that—but of a horse's neigh and wooden wheels on gravel, popping pebbles at Scribe's prized guinea hens. Those screeches of displeasure rang a few tones higher in her ears.

Darling straightened her frock, beating free the filth the feather mattress hadn't claimed onto the floor in dusty swoops. Particles of hay and feed and barnyard dust glistened in the few light beams that found their way between the smudges on the window. The dress was one of only three Darling owned. This one was one year—maybe two—too short, barely draping the bottom of her kneecaps. Tiny pink flowers dotted the collar and cuffs around the short sleeves. A touch her mother had added when the plain garb arrived at the mercantile. The dress had once been her prized possession.

Darling didn't have any such prized things now, and the dress would be worn at least twice more before she dared wash it for fear of wearing out the already sagging, thin hems.

Her worn-out leather sandals, six months too small, waited exhaustedly by the cutout to the first floor. She dropped each one down the hole and they landed with a plop. Apprentice didn't like that she did this. Told her it wasn't proper. But she'd caught her strap on one of the ladder's wooden rungs once and fell off backward onto her tailbone to the wood floor below. And she'd told him that she'd be worth very little broken and her family's debt would go unpaid. He'd held his temper after considering her observation. This time.

Other times, not so much.

At any rate, she'd climb the ladder up with her shoes on. But going down backward she accomplished barefoot. Her toes could feel the grip better than the too-small sandals. She positioned the ladder just so with slightly less sweaty palms than the job required when she first started. She'd been serving the Apprentice for so long that she should be used to the ladder. And the backward decline. Barefoot or shoed. She should be used to it.

But the fall and the height of the loft had other ideas and played havoc with her nerves.

And now, someone was conversing with Apprentice Scribe and she wasn't there to bring cool well water with the ladle and tin cup and offer the guest the fresh-baked cherry tarts she'd completed just a few hours ago. Another scolding was imminent. She'd be reprimanded for her absence. Her master never rested. Why should a lowly farmhand such as her nap? A prime youth, at fourteen, she should be full of energy. She'd heard these things from her mother before. And now Apprentice.

Before, in her old home, she'd sleep at midday to avoid her father's drunken rants. The higher the sun, the louder his voice. Seemed the rising of the sun higher in the sky sent her into survival sleep.

Now? Now the sleep was to make up for the dreamless hours of planning and prep at night. For that was the only time Darling's hands would stop shaking. When she knew he'd not sneak around some corner and find her in the midst of her plottings and devices.

She slipped her right foot into the right sandal and scooped up the left with her right hand and worked it on as she stumbled to the windowsill for the tarts. She smoothed her thick braid and tucked a curly strand of blond hair behind her ear. She loaded a tin plate with three tarts—two for the guest, one for Scribe, none for herself—and bounded out the door, nearly landing at Scribe's feet in a disheveled mess.

The visitor smiled at Darling. Tall and trim, he had the bluest eyes, like the middle of the pond when the clouds hadn't formed. His cheeks sprouted whiskers that had been trimmed a few days ago. Not enough to call a beard, but she imagined how scratchy they'd be if she were to run her fingers through them. She looked away, back to the Scribe who took the dish of tarts and wrinkled his caterpillar eyebrows at her. He nodded toward the well. She obliged.

Geese and ducks and those first-of-the-season spring offspring scattered around her as she ran for the water bucket. The guinea hens had already gone to the barn, pouting and puffed out over the white and gray horse. Down and feathers escaped the backs of the startled birds—always startled unless she held the feed bucket, and they always associated her with the feed bucket. The feathers floated around her feet. More work for her. Pick them all up. Inspect for quills. Always on the lookout for quills, even in her sleep. She'd stuff pillows and bedclothes with the softest remnants and the down that fell from the chicks' backs and bellies.

"They give us gifts. We ought not waste," the Scribe had instructed when she'd first arrived on his property.

She'd gotten creative. The first of her position to scour and pluck and not leave any feathers for the ground. And the Scribe hated seeing feathers on the ground. Wasteful. Those plumes that weren't fit for the parchment, but too pokey for the textiles? Well, she had other uses for those. And even Apprentice Scribe with all his other-worldly blessing of seeing, didn't know about her hiding place in the barn.

Darling attached the rope to the bucket's handle and positioned herself at the well so she could admire the visitor. Well, not admire. She was too young for such nonsense. Too much debt to work off before she could even think of such carefree frivolities. But a girl could dream, couldn't she?

He was much younger than the Scribe, this visitor. She'd not seen him here in the year she'd been indentured. His pants and shirt fit his frame and outlined muscles in his arms and legs. This man's clothing had no spots or stains. The Scribe, old enough by far to be Darling's father, always wore baggy trousers, baggy button-up shirt, and an apron all covered with ink. The men made quiet conversation while they snacked on the tarts. The visitor tucked his brimmed hat under his arm and retrieved parchment documents from a leather satchel in his buggy. Before he turned back to the Scribe, he ran his hand down the muzzle of his horse. Darling's heart melted at this tiny act of kindness.

The visitor showed the papers to the Scribe, who raised his voice and waved his hands in the kind man's face. She couldn't hear what her master said, but Darling's heart regained its position and beat a little faster as her palms sweated all over again. She wrestled the bucket up, gathered two tin cups and the ladle and waddled, embarrassed at her gait, back to the men.

"Forget that, Darling. He's not to drink from my well. He bears bad news and even a more sour tone of disrespect."

"Sir. I just bring the message. Master—"

"Master Seer is wrong. He's not been here himself in ages. He's not seen what measures I take to produce the documents he needs. I think his gift to be fading."

Startled at the Scribe's insult—one punishable by hanging should it ever be uttered by mere commoners—both Darling and the visitor took half-steps backward. Even a dozen or so of the white geese flapped in anxious discord and headed to the barn, their young waddling in suit.

"I'm sure you take great care." The visitor looked around the barnyard at all manner of feathered creature. "I can see you've got quite the supply. Perhaps something's happened with your skill level. Your lines aren't as thin. They aren't as crisp or clean." He leaned in close to the Apprentice and whispered, just loud enough for Darling to hear. "And your ink bleeds."

"Well, I never!"

"At any rate, Master Seer expects better products from you, or he'll have to find another Scribe."

The Apprentice took the water bucket and dumped it on the

ground, splashing some of it onto himself, before Darling could react. She took several startled steps away from the men. "Now, sir. Not in front of the young lady. Mind your manners."

"I'll not be told by young commoners how to behave in front of my keep." The Scribe brushed down his stained apron, now wet with well water. "What massive disrespect. You may leave, now, Jonathan." As he pointed to the visitor's horse and waved with the other hand, Darling saw Apprentice Scribe's palms. With simple well water, the stains on the apron transferred blues and reds onto his skin.

She suppressed a grin, lest she be backhanded. Well, what do you know? Apprentice Scribe's ink does indeed bleed.

Darling waited for her next orders as the visitor turned the buggy around in the barnyard and aimed his horse down the lane. Apprentice Scribe paced back and forth, the edge of his trousers kicking up tufts of feathers and down from the startled birds. The yard had been cleared before Darling's nap and would have remained so save for this ruckus. "I thought I told you not to waste. The yard is in dismay!"

"Yes, sir." Darling was about to apologize, but the yard was clear before the visitor—before Jonathan—arrived. No use arguing.

"And I need fresh ink." He looked at his hands, startled by the purple blending of hues. He wiped off a bead of sweat with his sleeve and his hands again on his apron, then snapped at her. "Bring it to me after you clean this mess up."

Darling collected the tin cups and empty tart plate and left them on the windowsill. She'd pull them into the house from the inside later. She returned to the well's stone ledge with the bucket and ladle. She managed to drip enough water into her mouth to wet her dusty lips and dampen the cotton blooming inside her cheeks. She didn't dare bring up fresh for herself. She'd have to wait until he got thirsty.

Her collection apron hung from a rusty stake driven into the side of the house. The Scribe had sewn it himself for his previous hand, so it, of course, was too small. Other scribes' hands had their family debts paid by Darling's age. Not her father's, debt though. She'd belong to Apprentice Scribe for many more seasons until she'd be forced to work naked or he'd have to order a new wardrobe.

She draped the strap around her neck and tied the strings in the back allowing the muslin to dangle over her dress. She started her scan of the yard. First by the well where she found tufts of down fit for his pillow. She tucked a handful's worth into the first pocket. Further into the yard, where the hens had retreated from the horse, she found two quills and six feathers not fit. She ran her fingers along the smooth edges as the soft barbs one by one returned to their rightful positions along the shaft. She'd need to trim one of them to allow the ink good flow. The other was fit as is. She carefully tucked these into a special pocket, sewn long and tall, in the middle of the apron.

Darling looked back to the house. The Scribe had gone inside. From the open door, she could see him sitting, his back slumped over the writing table in the corner by the fireplace. She quickly scooped the unfit feathers, and in one brisk motion, crammed them down the bodice of her dress. They poked and itched and tickled. But she was used to this. And it would only be until she could reach the barn and stow them away in her secret hiding place.

She continued her scour and scooping up of the barnyard until she was sure he'd not have reason to squawk at her. Until another duck or goose or hen decided to drop feather.

The barn was dim despite the afternoon sun. The barn on her home property was filled with windows all around, save for where the horses backed in. Their stalls were protected from the elements by cedar planks held to the frame with iron nails.

This barn wasn't meant for horses. Only fowl. A back door faced the rear of the property and the pond. This door stayed open for all the daylight hours to allow those birds who enjoyed swimming quick access from their wooden roosts to the water's edge. The front door faced the barnyard. The chickens and hens liked congregating here, as it was closest to where Darling kept the feed buckets. Two simple paneless windows, cut high above each door near the rafters, remained open to allow fresh air. Even in the coldest of nights, those windows were never shuttered.

Darling had worried about the birds. If she were lying in her feather bed shivering through the cold with a cast iron stove blazing heat below her, wouldn't the birds in the breezy barn be cold too?

"Do not shutter them. The birds are fine. One never knows when the Master Seer will send the special quills. You must check below these windows each morning for the Ural's gifts."

Ural's gifts. A black and white pristine quill from an owl longed for by every scribe, whether apprentices or not. The lines made with the tip were so fine, they were nearly invisible. And the seeing properties once such a quill met ink and parchment, well. Apprentice Scribe talked about this in his sleep. His moaning had brought Darling from her tiny loft one night—backward down the ladder and barefoot. She'd stood at the head of his bed as he tossed and wished and prayed for the owl to come. To bless him and his parchment with seeing beyond all that was currently possible with his meager abilities.

For him to be blessed by the gods to find such a quill as Ural's.

Darling topped the three lanterns by the door with fresh oil and lit each one carefully with a long-sticked match. She left one by the door and took the other two past rows and rows of nesting boxes, some nailed to the barn walls one on top of the other. Those were the hardest to muck. She hated ladders, and the top rows were almost impossible for her to reach. She was glad the current flock favored the lower nests. The Scribe had ordered the carpenter to build more boxes, which stood in freestanding rows in the middle of the floor, back-to-back and side-to-side, nearly fifty extra spaces for the birds to roost, mate, lay and drop quills.

She reached the workbench where the Scribe's ink press sat. The occasional quack or call escaped from the boxes behind her. Some birds waddled in from the pond. Some waddled out for their afternoon swim or the hope of a guppy or tadpole snack. Darling filled the basin of the copper drum with her master's special mixture. Glass bottles—some with droppers as stoppers, others with screw-on lids and wooden scoops the size of Darling's little finger—lined a cabinet shelf above the workbench. A shelf he locked tight once the sun started to set. None of the bottles were labeled with anything but tally marks. One drop of this. Three scoops of that. "Why not just name the bottles, that way—"

"I won't be told how to run my business. You've no need of knowing the ingredients. Each scribe has a special formula, keyed to his own abilities and gifts. Divinely prescribed by the Master Seer." He'd turned one of the bottles of powder over in his hand the day he'd shown her the press. "And, being a girl, what use would you have of words?"

Darling began assembling the ingredients, no longer needing the tally marks to guide the process. A few drops of this. A prescribed number of scoops for that. She screwed the copper top onto the drum and pulled down hard on the crank. Then back up again. Down and up. Up and down, until the glass ink well resting at the spout of the drum filled drip by drip of his fresh batch of dye.

Dye that was supposed to stain parchment pages with foretellings and fortunes and divine directions for the king and his men. Or for foul-hearted men looking to seek an easy way out of hard work.

Dye that wasn't supposed to run.

But this ink did. She smiled. Apprentice Scribe's journey was about to come to an end. She'd heard from her mother the fates of other scribes and seers who'd failed to make adequate batches. The gift of foresight fleeing their hands and their quills as quickly as it had been bestowed by the gods upon these men.

Her mother had prepped her as well as she could. She'd known for months that Darling would be taken away to pay the price of her father's misfortune. One of those foul-hearted men. One that brought their family great sorrow and great debt. Father had bribed a seer, one much more powerful than a simple apprentice scribe. A seer so powerful that, when he saw how wicked Father was being with the new money, he'd been able to reverse Father's good fortune with a few swift strokes of ink on parchment.

With a black and white quill from Ural.

She'd gotten a close look at that parchment. The one delivered by three kingsmen. The ink shimmered and sparkled on the bumpy animal hide. As they hauled her father away in the caged buggy, little

Darling remembered feeling sorry for the animal who'd given its covering to allow the seers and the scribes to do their work.

But not so sorry for her father.

Darling held back a tear. She'd not seen nor heard word of her family since the day the Scribe had sent for her. A man similar to Jonathan—though not nearly as kind or handsome—had loaded her and her couple of dresses and not much else onto his wagon and they'd ridden for hours with the clopping of the horses beating on her eardrums and the stench of the man's sweat filling her nostrils through the summer heat all those many miles to Apprentice Scribe's barnyard.

One more crank of the press and the fresh ink was ready. Darling held the glass up to the lantern's flame. Blues and reds swirled in perfect harmony. Not blending. Not bleeding.

At least not until they hit the Apprentice Scribe's parchment.

Darling had always admired the way the ink swirled in the bottle. The tiny sparks of magic embedded deep in each molecule shimmered now. They had shimmered and bounced off the Scribe's wooden tabletop as he drug the quills along the parchment. They've been shimmering less and less. Only in the bottle. Not so much on his parchment.

Maybe Jonathan was right. The Scribe was losing his power. Darling shuddered. She'd no idea what would become of the already thin veil between his temper and his actions should he well and truly become unworthy of the ink.

Yes, for months her mother had prepped her. Training her in all things—well, all things her mother knew—regarding Scribes and Seers and the Master. Teaching her to read. Darling had taken to words quite well. A task forbidden of women and girls, as the men believed lasses and ladies were more suited to maids and barn keeps. Darling's father had seen to it to teach his wife the basics after the Seer's parchment had brought him ill-fated fortune—along with so much misery. "You and Darling may need this skill someday. I fear I've made a grave error."

Darling had tried hard not to hate her father for his greedy itches. Every man had a right to dream, didn't he?

And if men could dream, why not women and girls?

Father was long gone and Mother burdened with the debt he'd left —a deep and magical one only the firstborn could pay off. Darling was the only heir, girl or not. She'd not see her mother in five more summers. Darling would be nearing twenty years old and truly unfit to wed at that old age. Mother had tried to spare Darling this servitude, spending so much time at the spinning wheel and with needle and thread in fingers that the weary woman had blisters and bloodstains. It simply wasn't enough.

So the lessons began. Learning. Reading. Training. Doing without. How to wear down a man with incessant talk and questions. And most importantly how to sense when a backhanded blow is heading your way.

These lessons of magic and words continued until the carriage came and took young Darling away. Mother had to be held by two strong men as her only child was loaded up and carted off to the Apprentice Scribe's land.

She shuddered again. By Ural's beak, she'd break free of this hold before it was too late.

Before her master well and truly realized Jonathan's warning as correct.

Before Darling was reduced to a heap of weary and battered bones atop a glorious bed of feathers.

Darling emptied her first apron pocket of the bedding fluff into a large bin under the workbench. It was two-thirds full. By this time next week, she could freshen the Scribe's pillows.

But by this time next week, well. Maybe not.

She placed the quills into a long, wooden box with a brass latch. Ural was carved on the lid. Apprentice Scribe was running low on those. Quills were always harder to find than fluff and unfits. True quills were precious.

Valuable.

She'd not realized until he'd taught her—her mother had no way of knowing this fact—that the only plumes fit for parchment were those from the left feathers—the shafts were angled just right for dragging the tips across the parchment. And not just any feathers from the left wing, the five at the end. The flight feathers. Other feathers would do in a pinch, but for the King and those who served the realm, Apprentice Scribe only wanted the best.

And one must never pluck the quills. They must be gifts from the fowls. "Magic isn't taken. It's given to and patiently awaited by those men who are truly deserving," Apprentice Scribe had told her the day a few months ago when he'd ran out of quills and was forced to use feathers unfit. He'd told her of evil men who'd gone so far as to net Ural and met their fates in the most cruel way. Impatient and undeserving every one.

But Darling wasn't patient. And Darling wasn't a man. But she certainly deemed herself deserving.

She closed the box and traced Ural's round head and big eyes and smiled as the unfit feathers pressed inside her bodice itched and poked. She reached inside for them and gave a quick look back to the house. Hens and ducks sauntered along, pecking at the ground. No movement. He was still inside. Still scribbling. No doubt hoping for shimmering sparks of magic to bounce as they once did months ago. Longing for the magic to linger a while longer. To harness enough of it to rid himself of the apprenticeship label—and of the glowering eyes of the King and Master Seer.

She found it amazing that the magic and Ural's kind had once deemed this man she labored for fit for the magic quill. Only so many men at a time could be scribes. And of all the men, he'd been one of them.

She pulled out the handful she'd hidden in her dress and pulled the bin of fluff from under the table. Quickly. She'd almost been caught twice, and on those occasions she'd slept with the unfit feathers pressed against her skin all night until morning when he was too busy with cherry tart breakfasts to care that she'd snuck to the barn. Here. Under the workbench. Behind the bin of fluff.

A muslin sack sewn in her loft from the apron scraps and mattress covers as he'd slept, she stuffed the unfits in with dozens of others gathered over the many months. She almost had enough. She felt deeper into the sack for the cool of the glass. Still there. Still intact. And though she didn't pull it out to inspect it, Darling pictured the ink swirling in the bottle she'd stolen from him. She'd made a double batch of ink three weeks ago. One for him. One for her. A risky move as the ink press and ingredients were locked up tight at night and she'd had to be quick with the press and the hiding. This couldn't be done at night as the key hung deep under the layers of Apprentice Scribe's apron and shirt. She was daring. But not that daring.

She was just waiting on that one quill. That one special flight feather from the tip of Ural's left wing. Any day now. He was due.

She removed her now-empty apron and slung it over her arm to return it to the spike in the wall. She approached carefully this man. This unpredictable, sometimes wise, but mostly scary man.

"Your new batch is ready, my lord."

He said nothing to her, just nodded to the edge of the battered tabletop. She gently placed the bottle at the corner, but away from his elbow. She'd learned that initial lesson quickly, the first day she'd placed a bottle near the edge, but too close to his elbow, and spilled an entire magical batch to the floor.

She reached up to brush that stray lock behind her ear again. She wondered if he's the reason that lock wouldn't stay put. The scar next to it he'd dealt her when the ink spilled. She'd seen it coming, but had no way to buffer that blow.

"Away with you. Clean the yard."

"But my lord, I've already—"

"Then check the pond. Check the forest's edge. I need more quills." He shouted that last bit and rose from the stool, toppling it behind him. Darling reached for the ink bottle just before his flailing arms could knock it to the floor. He raised the hand that still held the goose quill, dripping with ink that no longer shimmered, as if to strike her. Darling stepped back, holding the bottle. He stopped himself.

She held her breath.

He scowled at her. "None of this happened before. None of this,

this *weakening*. Not until you came." He threw the quill to the table, the edge of the parchment page soaking up and bleeding the hues across the fibers. "And tomorrow, once my wits have returned, tomorrow I count!" He stomped out of the house into the barnyard.

That was her cue. Randomly, Apprentice Scribe would count the glass jars and the ingredients to rest his mind of imagined thievery. As if the ducks and guineas and geese cared to waddle off with his stash.

As terrifying as it was, she'd been waiting for a moment such as this. A moment when he was away from the writing table in a huff or a hurry, leaving her unattended near an unlocked parchment. Clean and smooth and unmarred with his thin, shaky lines and bleeding ink. She snatched the fresh parchment still rolled with its frail leather strap from Scribe's supply cabinet—another of which a key hung from around the man's neck—and slipped it into her bodice. What a different sensation than prickling and tickling of feathers. The parchment seemed to meld to her skin, giving her assurance that her plan wouldn't fail, even though the sweat on her palms and the thudding of her heartbeat told her otherwise.

She prepared dinner for the man. Corn cakes and fish leather. She declined her meager portion, declaring a bellyache—which wasn't a lie—and requiring early retirement to her loft. He seemed relieved, for it was in the pre-dark hours that Darling would start chatting. Incessantly. Like her mother told her. Questions and comments and random ramblings of all manners. He brushed her off toward the ladder. She climbed it with her shoes on, stomped toward the feather bed and then tiptoed—shoes still on—back to the ladder's opening.

She laid on her stomach as he finished his ale by the fireplace. Then she heard him round the corner to his room, muffled footsteps and rustling of cloth and then...

Snores and moans.

Apprentice Scribe was finally asleep.

In the dark, she put on her smallest dress first, then the next smallest, then the largest, until she was layered in her only three pieces. Darling grabbed her candlestick and left the lantern, even though it would give her more light. She needed the wax and there was a lantern in the barn, but it, too would be included in his count as soon as the sun came up, so she'd likely take off in her sandled feet through the forest in the dark, only the stars and good luck to guide her.

She tucked the rolled parchment page between the bodice of dress one and dress two, and...

She took a deep breath as she turned her back to the ladder whole. With her shoes on.

The full moon, another blessed act of magical timing, attempted to assure her through the dingy windowpane as she tried to find that first rung without catching her strap.

One uneven wooden rung at a time.

Until she was drenched in sweat from dress layers and stress. She paused at the foot of the ladder in the silence. Too silent. Then, she exhaled once Apprentice Scribe let out a long, garbled snort from around the corner. He was still sleeping. She snatched a knife from behind the cookware—a move her mother told her to do as soon as Darling arrived. "Stash something sharp. Right away so it can't be blamed on you." The knife wouldn't be in tomorrow's count, as it was missing the first day she was there.

Darling undid the latch on the front door, stepped outside and closed the door behind her. In the morning, he'd think her out at the pond or the wood's edge looking for quills.

In the morning, when he finished his count, which would be just fine as Darling was taking nothing countable, he'd think her finding those prized quills and simply taking a bit to return.

In the morning, he'd be wrong.

She reached the barn and secured the door shut. A few of the birds tried to greet her despite the dark.

"Ssshh, my friends. It's only me." She was prepared to open the back door and throw out as much food as would keep the multi-specied flock busy while she finished her travel preparations, but the fowls must've had their fill between grain in the yard and fish at the pond. They soon settled back to sleepy coos and, for a few of the larger geese, snores louder than Apprentice Scribe's.

She relaxed as she felt over the shelf by the door for the match sticks. The moon's rays didn't reach the bottom of the barn at all and she lit the candle, its flame darted to life and danced, casting shallow shadows of the nesting boxes along the floor as she made her way to the workbench.

She knelt on the trodden earth by her stash. She pulled the feathers unfit and began to strip the barbs and clip the ends. When she'd completed this, she cleaned up the remnants and stuffed them into the bottom of the downy bin. Someone else would have to stuff Scribe's pillows. By the time the mess was discovered, Darling would be long gone.

She took the hollow shafts and, using them as a straw, dipped each one into the stolen bottle of ink. When her tongue registered the bile mixture, she slid her finger over the end of the quill in her mouth to prevent drips and dipped the free end into the wax. And she waited. She then took the candle and allowed a single drop of wax to seal the end of the shaft that had just been in her mouth. She filled tube after tube with ink until the bottle was nearly empty and her shaved-down, clipped feathers unfit were all used up. Sometimes she'd freeze and listen, straining to hear around the nesting box's residents and their sleep noises.

Did she hear him? Was the scribe awake?

After a few startles, she'd resigned herself that if he were awake and she were caught, it was all over for her. If not, she needed to keep going.

She sprinkled the last few drops of ink from the bottle onto the workbench—already stained from so many other fillings—and replaced the bottle in the line of empties. The count would be just right when the sun came up.

She wrapped the filled hollow quills and the parchment and the knife in her muslin sack and straightened her dresses around her knees. The barn went completely silent as another, louder rustle toward the back of the barn kicked up. Up high. A call, long and low and soft at the same time.

Darling looked up. A few of the birds poked their long necks from their boxes.

He'd come. In the full moon. In just the right time. Ural had come.

"Please, Ural. You've been watching. I know you've been watching over me. Or I'd not have survived this long."

Ural turned sideways, his left side facing her, his right free to the starry sky. He flashed his round eyes and spread his magnificent wings as if daring to leave. As if daring her to keep pleading.

But Darling would beg no more. She was either deserving.

Or she wasn't.

The glorious owl spread his wings, his silhouette outlined against the black sky by the white of the moon. And he shuddered his feathers violently before disappearing out of the rafter window and into the night.

A painful sob welled in Darling's chest, but she brought a hand to her mouth and swallowed hard as she realized what Ural had done. A single, left-winged flight feather floated and twirled and twisted in the stale barn air. She scampered as it darted in the drafts. She didn't want it to reach the ground, all trampled with webbed prints and tufts of fluff and excrement. She caught it in midair.

She wanted this feather to remain pristine until the time came to dip the glorious tip into the ink and scroll out her own fortune with lines so smooth and thin they would be barely visible.

To write in unbleeding ink a fortune that included a home for her. For Mother—if her mother was still alive.

One where Darling, the first female Seer, would help those less fortunate instead of selling out to the scoundrels in the king's court.

Perhaps one that included a white and gray horse and his kind owner named Jonathan.

YOUR FRIENDLY NEIGHBORHOOD PHARMACY

When an errant pharmacy dispenses an unwanted drug, Tristan is understandably perplexed. But unwanted and unneeded are not the same thing, and Tristan might live to regret his decisions... or not.

ristan Lee slammed the contents of his suit jacket onto his dresser after a long day at the office. The phone didn't stop ringing. All. Day. Long. He splashed water on his face and looked at his graying mop in the mirror, hair growing increasingly lighter and looser by the month.

In college, Tristan had dreamed of creating a base of clients that he could take from zero to hero—financially speaking—but what he'd gotten was a bunch of whiny middle-aged men who hadn't planned for their futures and now wanted Tristan to be their rainmaker with little capital and even less time.

Friday afternoon had come none too soon. He tossed off his suit and left it crumpled on the closet floor of his single bedroom sublet with a bad view of a brick wall across the street. The only time the view changed was when the neighborhood hoodlums graffitied over the painted mess they'd made the weekend before. Last weekend it was a red devil with purple horns and some scrawl above its head he couldn't quite make out.

He tugged on his jeans and threw on a twice-worn T-shirt that would pass if he put on extra deodorant and cologne. He pulled the bedroom shade, letting the fabric roll too far into the roller.

The devil was still staring at him.

The kitchen cabinets were bare of anything but condiments since his sixty-plus hours this week had afforded him little time to grocery shop. He opened the fridge and was greeted by half a tub of margarine, milk past the date by a week, and a sliver or two of lunch meat that had gone green around the edges. He slammed it shut.

He couldn't even make it rain for himself.

The hollow in his stomach demanded attention. He retrieved his wallet and keys and as he was reaching for his cell, it flashed that he'd missed a call. He let out a groan and flipped open the voicemail app. He didn't recognize the number, so it wasn't an active client, which was a relief. He pressed the playback button.

"Voicemail from Friday afternoon." He needed to change that setting, but he always got sidetracked and never got it done.

A recorded voice, robotic and masculine, greeted him. "Hello. This is your friendly neighborhood TriMart Pharmacy. You have one new prescription ready for pickup."

Tristan most certainly didn't have anything ready for pickup. He hadn't been to the doctor in three years and his last prescription had been for the clap five years ago. He deleted the message. An incompetent pharmacy tech likely put the wrong number in for one of their patients. He would ignore it, but then he laughed out loud at the thought of some old geezer going without his little blue pills. He shook his head. He was one sick, overworked puppy.

TriMart was only a couple blocks away, and they had a small deli and grocery section. He'd let them know about the error so they could contact the correct person.

~

"Next."

Tristan had waited in line behind three people to speak with the tech. Several blue-smocked workers ran back and forth in the tiny pharmacy, bumping into one another. Their phones rang off the hook. No wonder they'd made a screw-up. He wouldn't be surprised if in all the chaos someone walked out with something that could kill them.

He approached and spoke to the young woman through a speaker embedded in the window. A half-moon shape in the glass gave way to a stainless steel well in the counter for the exchange of money and prescriptions. Someone had tried to rob them at gunpoint a few months back, according to the papers.

"May I help you?" The brunette adjusted her smock and readied her fingers over the computer's keyboard. "Brandi" was etched in blue onto the white nametag hanging from her lapel.

"Yeah, Brandi," Tristan said in his nicest, most patient voice. The fake one he used with some of his best clients. "There seems to be a mistake." Tristan explained the message.

"Okay, what is your date of birth?"

"Can't you just look it up by my phone number? That's the error. You've got the wrong number."

"Well, we always start with date of birth."

Tristan shifted his weight and decided to play along. They had a scripted, methodical protocol. No way Brandi was gonna cave on it. She typed in his date and smiled.

"You have one script ready. Just a moment."

"No, no no. I don't. It's not mine, that's what I'm trying to tell you. I haven't had anything filled here for years."

The girl hesitated. She returned to the screen. "Well, let's confirm your address."

Tristan huffed and obliged.

"Let's see. There's the script from today, and then there was…" She hit a few more keys, her eyes widened and her cheeks flushed red. "And there was one from a few years back."

Now Tristan shifted his weight for an entirely different reason. "Look, I don't have a script. It belongs to someone else. I'm only trying to tell you so whoever it belongs to can be notified."

"Oh, I see. Hold on a minute." Brandi spun around to speak with her boss, the pharmacist who stood behind a tall counter off to the side. Tristan profiled him while he waited. Nearing retirement. Made a sweet yearly salary. Probably had less than half of what he and his family would need to retire on comfortably. And only if the rest of his days were filled with an easy-going and mundane lifestyle.

The white-coated gentleman approached the glass holding a white bag folded over at the top and stapled closed with a TriMart brochure. "Mr. Lee, you actually do have a prescription ready, and by law we must dispense it to you. There's no charge, as your insurance has covered the cost." He slid the baggie under the glass.

Tristan pushed it back. "You've got to be kidding me. I haven't been to the doctor or had a prescription for years. It can't be mine."

The line was growing impatient behind him. A shady character with body odor leaned toward him and whispered, "If you don't want it, I'll take it. Whatever it is."

Tristan shrugged him off as the pharmacist pushed the baggie through the window for the second time.

"Well, can you at least tell me what it is? I can ask questions about *my* medication, right?"

"Yes, of course." The druggist checked the computer screen. "Looks like HCTZ. That's the acronym for this medication. It's a water pill. Take it in the morning with a full glass of water and follow up with your doctor for repeat blood work in three months. You can sign the touchscreen pad to your right showing you picked up the medication. There's no charge today." He nodded to the payment machine, and Tristan played along. His stomach was rumbling and his patience was growing thinner by the moment.

He left the pharmacy window, grabbed some food staples and walked the three blocks back to his apartment in total exasperation.

THE FOOD HELPED with the anger and the cobwebs. He chased two ham sandwiches with a tall glass of fresh milk and killed a half can of Pringles while he watched the local news.

The prescription bag was still lying on the counter, taunting him. He should try to take it back tomorrow and see if there would be different staff on for the weekend, but his curiosity got the better of him. He ripped open the baggie and dumped the bottle into his palm. He turned it over and inspected it. Hydrochlorothiazide with HCTZ in parentheses. His name in the corner of the label. Unbelievable. The prescribing physician was the exact man who'd treated him for clap all those years ago.

Tristan took the bottle to the sofa and slumped down. He poured the tiny orange pills into his hand and then returned them to the bottle. He punched the name of the drug into Google on his phone and confirmed the water pill information the pharmacist had given him.

He was tired to the bone from the work week, and this escapade had sent him further into exhaustion. A guy tries to do the right thing.

He flipped open the trash can lid, tossed in the bag, brochure, and bottle, and turned off the kitchen lights.

The street lights started their nightly routine, turning on one at a time into the distance down the street in either direction. Tristan went to the bedroom window and wrestled with the roller shade. As he pulled it half way down, he noticed the updated graffiti in the alley's street lamp. A waterfall cascaded over a rocky cliff into a flaming hell.

And the devil danced at the bottom of it all.

TRISTAN SWUNG his legs over the edge of the bed and stretched. He'd slept harder and further into the morning than he had in a long time. He planned to start his Saturday with a jog and a late breakfast down at the diner. Then he would catch up on paperwork in front of the TV with intermittent breaks for laundry duty in the basement.

As he stood, he felt a strange sensation in his left foot, and he rotated his ankle a few times to try to remedy it. His ankle felt stiff and swollen. He sat down and took off his socks. His left foot was massively swollen. He couldn't remember injuring it, and he'd never seen his feet do that before.

He took a few laps around his apartment and, though the swelling didn't subside, the sensation of fullness lessened. After his shower, he weighed himself. Up five pounds from two weeks ago. The steady diet of Hot Pockets and chip lunches on the go had to stop. He dressed and put on his shoes. His left one was snug, but the strange swelling was subsiding.

Outside, the air was hot and humid. He took a deep breath, stretched out and started toward the school district about a mile away. After a couple of blocks, he couldn't tell there was anything wrong with his ankle, and the incident was quickly forgotten.

At the school grounds, he paused for another stretch near the water fountain and was about to take off again when his phone rang.

He fished it out of his gym shorts but didn't get it answered before it went to voicemail.

He clicked the playback button. "Voicemail from Saturday morning." He rolled his eyes at his lack of ability to take care of irritations when they were right in front of him.

"Hello. This is your friendly neighborhood TriMart Pharmacy. You have one new prescription ready for pickup."

You have got to be kidding. Tristan sank to a bench and wiped the sweat with the edge of his t-shirt. TriMart must be run by the biggest conglomeration of fools on the planet. He caught his breath, drank deep from the playground's fountain and jogged the mile and a half to TriMart.

An entirely new set of staff worked behind the pharmacy's glass. He gave the blue-smocked tech, Stacy this time, his vital statistics right up front to save time. He could smell the soured t-shirt and body odor and was glad for the barrier.

Stacy smiled. "Looks like you have one ready, Mr. Lee. And no charge. Your insurance has paid for the balance."

Tristan would have to call his insurance company next week and make them stop paying for scripts he didn't need. It may constitute some sort of fraud, and he couldn't afford to lose his coverage, even if he rarely used it. He didn't have time to mess with this.

"There's been a mistake. That's not mine. I've not seen Dr. Baker for quite some time—"

"Well, he called this one in last night after hours. We just filled it this morning."

"What is it this time? Tell me it's something good. At least something with some street value." Tristan was irate.

"Mr. Lee, we take those kinds of statements seriously. I'd not joke about that." Stacy retrieved the bag and slid it under the glass.

Tristan opened it up right there. HCTZ. Same idiotic thing as yesterday.

"Do you have any questions for the pharmacist?"

"Oh, I have a lot of questions for the pharmacist." He rattled the bottle at the window and Stacy retrieved an attractive lady in a white coat.

"His info is already on the screen." Stacy retreated to the back, and the pharmacist examined the screen.

"Looks like he called you in a dose increase, Mr. Lee. How's your swelling?"

Tristan took a step back, the morning's issue with his ankle surfaced above his irritation. "How did you know about that?"

"Well, this medication is usually prescribed for mild water retention or blood pressure issues. With a dose increase so close to the first script, I'm assuming you had trouble with swelling last night and Dr. Baker ordered the increase."

Tristan stared at the lady in disbelief.

"Mr. Lee?"

"Yeah, okay." He signed the pad at the window, put the bottle in his pocket, tossed the baggie on the floor and stomped away.

TRISTAN'S cold shower and diner lunch did little to help calm him down. Both of his feet were so swollen by the time he reached the diner that he had to unlace his sneakers. This created more anxiety than he had the energy to deal with. The new bottle of pills rattled in his jeans.

"Can I get you anything else, sweetheart?" His senior citizen waitress, another poor soul who hadn't planned for her financial future, stood with his check in one hand and a sweaty pitcher of ice water in the other.

"Just a refill." He nodded to his water glass.

He wriggled the bottle out of his pocket. Same information on the label as before. Same doctor. Different strength, upped by twenty milligrams.

This was insane. It was all in his head. What was that called, when med students were studying for their exams and they started manifesting real symptoms of whatever quirky illness they learned about?

That's what it was. He didn't have swelling until he was told he had medication for it. Then the swelling got worse after the dose was updated, because his mind was playing tricks on him.

He threw money on the table for the check and a decent tip and on his way out the door, he tossed the bottle into the trash can.

He spent the rest of the day doing what he'd planned: paperwork, laundry and a steady intake of bad cop show reruns. Around ten p.m. he decided to turn in. He made a mental note to purchase a new shade for the bedroom tomorrow and eliminate one more area of frustration. In the street lamp below his bedroom, he could see the graffiti had been updated once again. The hoods must've run into extra cash for paint this weekend. And a ladder.

A weary-looking skeleton, at least ten feet tall, danced over hot coals. Evil black insects swarmed around his head and near his hands and feet. The same likeness of the devil, red-faced and purple-horned, danced with it and seemed to encourage the bony figure along the wall. The level of detail was amazing. Someone should hire the artist to do something productive with his life.

He finally managed to loosen the shade and fell into bed.

SUNDAY MORNING, the cell phone pulled Tristan from dreams of paperwork and being late for work. He brushed his eyes and grabbed the noisy thing. Two missed calls and two voicemails.

One from a frantic client that he'd deal with tomorrow morning.

The other from TriMart. He deleted the message without listening. This was ridiculous. He wasn't about to get involved again. Tomorrow morning, before dealing with the client, he'd call his doctor and the insurance company and put a stop to the whole mess. The TriMart people certainly weren't listening.

He swung the quilt off the bed and inspected his feet. The swelling was gone, as was the stiffness. He chuckled to himself and went about his morning.

TriMart called while he was in the shower. Again, he deleted the message without listening. They called during breakfast and once more during lunch. He finally blocked the number.

He kept his irritation at bay by keeping busy through the afternoon. He folded the laundry from yesterday and cleaned the shelves in the fridge. He made a shopping list of healthy foods and packable lunches and remembered the roller shade.

He rummaged through the bottom of the coat closet for his tool box and brought out the measuring tape. He measured the length and width of the bedroom shade, but before he could put the tape down and raise the shade, someone rang the doorbell.

He was greeted by a zit-faced twenty-something with a TriMart patch sewn onto a blue vest.

"Oh, no. I didn't order anything, and I'm not taking whatever it is that you have." Tristan tried to shut the door, but the delivery kid put his foot in the way.

"The pharmacist said you'd be a pain, but this one is important. I gotta leave this here with you no matter what, or they'll fire me." He shoved the white baggie folded over and stapled with the TriMart brochure into Tristan's gut. "No charge today."

Before Tristan could reply, the kid was halfway down the hall to the stairwell. He stood there in the doorway turning the package over in his hand. This one felt different than the first two. It didn't have a rattling bottle of pills, but something long and cylindrical.

He took it to the kitchen, ripped open the top of the baggie and dumped the object onto the counter. He recognized it immediately.

His girlfriend in college had had nut allergies and she'd carried an injectable like this in her purse everywhere she went. On one of their dates, Tristan even had to jam the thing into her thigh after a restaurant served her salad with slivers of almonds hidden among the romaine.

Tristan had no allergies whatsoever. He grinned, opened the syringe, pulled back the plunger and emptied the entire contents of the injectable into the kitchen sink and rinsed it all away. He tossed the mess into the trash and returned to the bedroom.

He opened the fickle shade one last time. And, as a solid goodbye to the pain in the ass, he let the thing up with a loud swish and flap as the fabric rolled around the top of the window. He turned to grab the grocery list and window measurements and stuffed the list into his pocket. He almost missed the new graffiti. Almost.

Never had Tristan seen the wall across the alley change so quickly. Once or twice a month, maybe every weekend, but never had he seen the artwork change daily. Maybe there was some sort of project in the community to keep the kids busy doing this sort of thing. He'd heard of programs like that, but this alley wasn't well-traveled and few would see the display.

He opened the window pane to get a better look. He leaned onto the window sill and poked his head all the way out. The skeleton from last night lay in a mess of flames and gray billowing smoke, his bottom half ashes, the top half melting away. The devil danced away, insects with giant stingers and sharp wings swarming over his head and around his hands like he was the Pied Piper of Hamelin.

As Tristan moved to close the window, he noticed the wasp's nest in the upper corner of the frame. He tried to shut the pane quickly, but the angry beast nailed him in the crook of the arm with a searing sting. Travis slapped it dead, its innards spreading on his arm. He ran to the bathroom to run water over the area. After the bug parts washed away, he could still see the butt of the thing pulsating in his arm. He tried to pull it out, but only got bits of it. The stinger was still inside him.

He pulled open drawers and the medicine cabinet searching for the tweezers, but couldn't find them. He tried scratching the stinger out with his fingernails, but the thing seemed to go in deeper. Redness from the puncture was now several inches around in all directions.

He dug and dug at it, and now the stinger was totally embedded. In only a few minutes, his entire elbow had swollen so that he couldn't bend it without severe pain.

His heart raced, and sweat beaded across his lip and forehead.

Then he remembered the delivery from TriMart.

He stumbled to the kitchen, the redness and pain now extended to his shoulder.

He knocked over the trash can and found the allergy pen. He jammed the thing into his arm, and pressed in the plunger, but it barely moved.

Swelling up to his neck now. It was getting hard to breathe. The walls of his small apartment seemed to shiver and move in close.

He dug his phone from his pocket, slid to the kitchen floor and fumbled with one hand to try to dial 9-1-1, but he dropped it. He could barely see the screen.

He slumped into a heap on the cool vinyl. Shakes and tremors racked his body. He reached for the phone again and jabbed at the screen, hoping to make contact with someone, anyone. He couldn't see. His breathing shallowed.

One last attempt with the phone.

The cell sprung to life. "Voicemail from Sunday evening."

"Hello. This is your friendly neighborhood TriMart Pharmacy. Thank you for being our valued customer. Your account has been closed."

THE RECRUIT

For Maranda, a foster child cycling through the system, it's hard holding onto any one family, not least because they need her to protect them—and protect them she will, even if it means setting fire to a house or destroying city property. After all, when the silent war is done, they will be there to guide humanity to a brighter future of symbiosis...

*M*y foster parents will send me to the State home soon. I know this because the birds' songs changed after the tree trimmers showed up several days ago. After three summers in a row, I can hear it in their voices clearly now—the light-hearted chirping of one mate calling to another, "All is well and please bring another worm" morphs into mournful calls of "the fledglings are dead and we have no home."

And if the birds have no home, neither do the Samin.

I start packing my red duffel with the broken zipper after the first round of bucket trucks and chipper machines pull onto the street to clear the electrical lines of impeding limbs. I pack up my few pieces of winter clothing first. I won't be staying with the Mathesons long enough to see the first snowflake. I pack the photos next. Me, smiling with the Marshalls and me again, smiling with the Perettis. Each family was kind enough to give me a frame to put the five-by-seven memento in a few months after I arrived with them. But always, always, the birds' songs change and I must do something to thwart my progress in the foster home.

While the grownups were busy fighting wars with countries and cultures and causes, their babies and teens, me included, became orphans. Orphans that taxed the already struggling social service system to the brink. Many families stepped up to house us, God bless them, and some just can't understand why we don't seem to behave and be grateful for a roof over our heads and three meals a day.

And while no one was looking, *they* came. They saw an opportunity and took it upon themselves to recruit a few of us. A few of us with no real roots. With no ties, now that our parents are dead. And no aunts or uncles or cousins to take us in. They recruited those of us still young enough—or sensitive enough—to hope in the fantastical.

To believe what they tell us.

To understand them.

I stuff the duffel under the twin bed the Mathesons graciously provided. My heart aches and I know I'll miss them the most. Their daughter, five years younger than me, reminds me of the little sister I lost in the bomb that also took my parents. The bomb that sent me into the move-or-die cycle of the Samin.

The last time I was sent back to State, Jesse, another girl about my age, had *that* look about her. At the time I didn't recognize it.

Now I do.

Jesse's foster family had sent her back after just two weeks. *They* were in danger and had asked her for help. She'd obliged by putting down the family's cat and setting their prize AKC Boxer loose on the highway. The social workers put us in a therapy group together because, well, we were troublemakers. Her with the pets, me with the fire at the Perettis' home.

Jesse's group is called the Yosni. She confided in me after I flat-out asked her, and flat-out broke the promise I'd made to the Samin. The promise to never reveal their existence under threat of death—or worse—to myself or to the foster families that housed me. The Yosni had made Jesse promise the same. But oh, well. What could they do? They needed us to survive.

I grab my journal, take the steps down two at a time and go to the back yard under the twisted branches of the giant hedge apple tree, one of the trees lining the perimeter of the yard that the trimmers haven't reached yet, but soon. The black powerlines snake through the leafy green, bending with the tree each time the breeze blew.

Of all the back yards I've visited, this is my favorite. The tree trunk twisted and turned and created a perfect nook for sitting and working in my journal. It's where the Samin give me the next set of directions. It's also where Kani, the barn owl that the Samin use to keep tabs on me, prefers to light. He's chosen a favorite branch high enough to watch me and remain hidden from all else. Many pages of my journal are devoted to him. I'd like to think of him as my guardian angel, but he's far from it.

I often wonder what Kani gets out of the deal.

The instructions come in whispers, and I jot down some notes. I take a deep breath. This will be the last time I sit in this tree. I'll miss it. I put the finishing touches on Kani's latest sketch.

I wonder whether Jesse's end of town is going through the same trimmings, or some other issue, like the blight that took out the pines at the Perettis.

Mr. Matheson hangs out the back door. "Maranda, time for dinner!" I close the leather-bound journal, the one my dad never got to use for his own art, and tuck the sketch pencils into my pocket.

Meatloaf, steaming mashed potatoes and corn on the cob oozing with butter. A fine last dinner with a fine family. We eat and make small talk about war and weather.

All the while my heart breaks.

I retreat to my room and look through my sketches. I spent hours drawing Jesse's hands. It was good practice, and aside from counseling sessions and chores, there wasn't much to do at State. She has the prettiest hands I've ever seen, despite the scars on her wrists.

Tonya, though. Tonya's eyes still haunt me. Green and empty and full at the same time. The orderly said she might have schizophrenia. Jesse and I tried to connect with her last fall. Tried to find out if she was a Recruit. It's hard to tell. Her thoughts made sense, then they didn't. But neither would mine if I spoke them aloud.

A minuscule race of not-quite-humans live in the treetops and demand my protection.

I don't even believe the words. Some days it makes me nearly crazy.

Maybe they did recruit Tonya.

I wait until the Mathesons fall asleep. I throw on my black hoodie and retrieve a flashlight, hammer, nail and wire clippers from Mr. Matheson's toolbox in the garage and slip out the side door.

The tree trimmers left their heavy equipment a block down the street. Town residents, grateful for their service to keep the grid up as best as possible after the fires and bombings, grateful for the power and even spotty Wi-Fi, allow the company to park their vehicles and bucket trucks anywhere they like.

The trees around the Matheson's home will be next. Probably tomorrow afternoon at the latest. If the trimmers reach the hedgeapple trees, the Samin's home will be destroyed.

The Samin told me, like the Yosni told Jesse, that if humans could learn symbiosis, the wars would be unnecessary. Their kind understand it well, at least among themselves. Symbiosis was learned over centuries with the birds and squirrels and the occasional raccoon. House pets, not so much. Humans, especially adult humans, not so much.

I puncture the tires. I clip wires. It would give the Samin another day or two to relocate. I'm pretty sure I'll get caught. Stealth isn't my strong suit.

If I'm caught, State will take me back and relocate me. Somehow, the Samin always know where I'll be and they're waiting with subtle greeting at the new foster home.

If I don't get caught, the Samin will go underground until the trees are trimmed, mourn the loss of their microscopic homes, and then rebuild.

If I fail, they run out of time to relocate. Then they die.

A porch light goes on across the street. And then another nearer to me. And then Mr. Matheson yells my name.

Too bad. Maranda Matheson sure would've had a nice ring to it.

The Mathesons once asked to see my drawings after witnessing me spending so much time sitting in the hedge apple tree. I carefully obliged because *they* were watching.

Mrs. Matheson told me I was incredibly talented, that I should submit the drawings to a gallery once the war was over. Or illustrate fantasy books.

But the sketches are far from fantasy.

They represent my current reality. And someday, when the grownup wars are over, and when the Samin and the Yosni, and others like them make their presence known, my sketches won't be illustrations in children's books.

They'll be the first-hand source of the new history books, hot off the presses.

When the current war is over, a new one will begin.

But *they* must survive until then.

THE BIBLIOPHILE'S CURSE

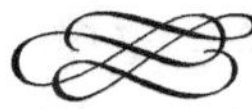

Given a rare opportunity to read an antique manuscript at his library, a rich book-lover jumps at the chance to handle an original 18th-century book destined for a museum. It's not every day one gets to read such ancient tomes, after all. But shortly after touching the pages, things take a turn for the worse...

lynn O'Hare arrived at Franklin Metropolitan Library precisely at five p.m. The library's one-hundred-year anniversary celebration ended at eight o'clock this evening. The gentlemen in black tuxes and ladies in colorful evening gowns danced and mingled in the library's main hall with its vaulted glass ceilings. The lighting was such that you couldn't see the stars, but the moon made its presence known, reflecting off the angles in the glass.

The library had invited five special guests, twenty-four-year-old Flynn one of them, to choose among five texts to peruse for a few hours. At midnight, the antiquities specialists would crate the priceless books in hermetically sealed containers and ship them to the British Library, where they would be displayed next to such marvels as the Gutenberg Bible, Beowulf, and Da Vinci's notebook. There, the five books would be housed under glass for the foreseeable future.

This was a once-in-a-lifetime experience. Flynn had tossed and turned every night for two weeks wondering which of the five texts he would be lucky enough to spend a few hours with. The chilly October evening matched the library's temperature, as earlier in the day the archivists had insisted they turn on the air conditioner to remove any trace of humidity for the sake of the texts.

He'd chosen his attire for the evening based on this fact, and the fact that he wanted to be comfortable for his reading session. He'd thought he might have to have his picture taken, but no flash photography would be permitted, so he put that fear to rest. He had settled on a long-sleeved orange polo, black jacket and jeans.

He imagined his anticipation was what one might feel when preparing for a long-awaited romantic meeting with a sweetheart, but he could only imagine. He'd spent far more time with books than with people, much to the chagrin of his family.

His stomach was killing him.

He fretted over the jeans a little, then decided not to worry too much about etiquette. No one paid attention to him anyway until he started throwing money around, which is how he'd received his gold-embossed invitation in the first place. His sizeable donation from his family inheritance would add an entire wing to expand the library's rare book and manuscript collection.

And every penny would be worth it.

Flynn stood to the side of the dance floor, nodding and smiling at couples and the library staff. One couple twirled by him, and he could make out the same perfume his mother had worn years ago, but he felt nothing at the aromatic memory.

He watched the massive clock above the stage tick away the time to the orchestra's last song, when the masses would exit and he could finally retreat to his assigned table and immerse himself in the book currently housed under lock and key somewhere in the basement.

Flynn's heart skipped and a bead of sweat formed on his forehead while extra security trickled into the crowd as the main festivities closed. Armed guards would grace each exit and another would patrol the reading tables while the five lucky patrons enjoyed the rest of their evening.

The last couple soon left the building, and a stern-faced security specialist supervised Dr. Sparks as he locked the massive front door. The antiquities specialist and the old librarian approached the five individuals standing in the middle of the hall.

"Welcome, welcome, and thank you each one so very much for your generous donations. Are you ready for your reward?" Dr. Sparks shook the men's hands and kissed the ladies on the cheeks.

Smiles and nods all around and anxious glances between the five. Flynn knew they were all hoping for the same thing—to be the first to choose among the five texts. He knew it shouldn't matter; all of them were sure to be magnificent. But still he wanted first dibs. He ran a hand through his shaggy blond hair. His stomach churned and flopped.

"The conditions of zis encounter were spelled out in your invitations, but vee vill go over zem once more before vee begin." The thick German accent of the gray-haired antiquities man lacked all emotion.

"First, zere vill be no food or drinks in zee reading area. You may not pick up zee manuscripts. You must remain seated. You must keep your gloves on at all times and refrain from touching your skin, face, hair or clozing. Your hands must remain on zee table at all times. You may not use extra lighting from cell phones, cameras or other devices. Only the provided table lamps are to be used. If you leave zee reading area, your session vill end and your manuscript vill be removed from zee area..."

Flynn's stomach let out a giant rumble, and he felt acid work its way up to the back of his throat. Something was wrong, not just a bad case of nerves. The librarian's assistant, Gloria, noticed he was having trouble. "Do you need to excuse yourself? You're awfully pale. We'll be sure to wait on you to get started," she whispered. "I'll explain it to them."

"That would be amazing." Flynn backed away from the group and turned for the restroom. He could hear the German and the head librarian going on with instructions and affirmations of what a rare opportunity this was.

In the bathroom, he relieved himself, washed his hands and splashed his face. He cupped his hand under the faucet and brought up a small bit of water, enough to wet his mouth. He wasn't sure what would happen if he drank anything right now. He couldn't spend all night in the bathroom.

When he returned, Gloria met him halfway to the reading tables, panicked. "I tried, Mr. O'Hare, I tried to stop them, but..." She looked over her shoulder.

The other four guests each sat at a different table. Each table held a small green-globed lamp. Manuscripts of differing sizes and thicknesses lay spread out before them. Flynn would get the leftover tome. The guard and the German ambled back and forth, one in front of the tables, one behind.

"It's okay, Gloria. Really. It couldn't be helped." The words came out, but he didn't mean them.

She showed him to his table. The German nodded to the pair of white gloves next to the blue, ragged book, and Flynn slipped them onto his slender hands. They were two sizes too big. He brushed his left hand over the cover of the book but couldn't make out the title at all. He gently opened the spine and let it lay flat on the table, careful to keep his right hand out of his lap and away from his chin and out of his hair—a nervous habit he hadn't known he had until that moment when he wasn't allowed to act on the impulse.

The title page was badly faded, but he was relieved it was in English. He could make out one name in the byline: Grimm. He could also make out the date at the bottom of the page: 1702.

The stoic antiquities expert reached Flynn's table and smiled for the first time all evening. "Zis one is my favorite. Zee ozers left it behind because zey couldn't read the title, but it's from my family line over 300 years ago." He puffed his chest out and ran a wrinkled hand over his necktie. His fingers fumbled with the tie tack. Flynn made out a black wolf with scarlet eyes on the gold piece. "Vell, at least a distant branch of my family line."

Flynn left both of his hands on the table, not yet turning the page. "It's in English."

"Ja. A translation. A descendant of Shakespeare fell in love with zee Grimms' tales and wrote zem in English."

Flynn lifted a few pages by the corners, peeked inside and frowned. "The Brothers Grimm lived in the late 1700s. They weren't even born when this was supposedly written."

"Extensive tests have confirmed zee age. And it's not zee Brothers, Mr. O'Hare. It's zee great-uncles of zose brothers." Flynn thought he saw the German wink. "Enjoy zee text, Mr. O'Hare. I'll leave you to it." He tapped his golden wolf tack once more and walked away.

Flynn's heart and stomach were thumping in time with one another. The *Uncles* Grimm! He gingerly opened the book to the first text page. An intricate illuminated letter B, three inches high and half as wide, began the first paragraph halfway down the page. The artwork was superb, rivaling anything he'd seen in any archival document or photo, and he'd never seen anything like it in a translation.

The B stood out in royal blue against a shimmering gold and emerald background of fleurs- de-lis. He ran his gloved thumb over the raised art and wished terribly that he could truly feel it. He got his face as close as he dared with the patrols walking back and forth and could make out the smallest of crimson serpents crawling up the letter, weaving in and out of green vines twisted around the shape of the letter. They weren't snakes or dragons or any lizard he'd ever seen, but they *were* reptilian. The intricate details played tricks on his eyes, weaving and bobbing the serpents through the holes of the letter, scales shimmering, slim claws grasping.

It wasn't until he pulled his nose back that he actually read the first word.

Beware.

Beware the tales told within. Read on with caution and trepidation.

Flynn arched his back and stretched his arms up, remembering the hair thing in time as he brought his hands back to the table. He was excited now, and wished he could remove his jacket, but that would require removal of the gloves and forfeiting the opportunity to continue reading. He glanced at the time. It was already 10:30. How long had he been staring at that letter?

Flynn adjusted the oversized gloves, which kept slipping down his hands. He flipped through the pages carefully, looking for the beginning of the next chapter, but couldn't find it. He was hoping to see another illuminated character but had no such luck. He allowed the pages to come to rest back at the beginning, and as they fanned into place, he could smell the ages of time on the book. How many hands had this been through before the museum found it? How many children had enjoyed the tales within? Flynn was almost ecstatic and had to work hard to remain seated.

He continued reading.

We told you to beware. The Woskits are everywhere. Stealing the breath of the young and creating turmoil for the mothers.

He read down the rest of the page of the terror at the hands—or claws—of the Woskits. As he was about to turn the page with his left hand, his right went straight through his hair. A wave of horror tore through him, causing his heart to stop for a full three seconds until he realized that no one had seen him. He was too worried about the right hand now contaminated with hair and oil to realize the left hand had worked its way out of its glove and his bare skin was resting on the gold-plated B.

He snatched the loose glove off the table and worked it back on, still unnoticed by the patrol. For the second time that night, sweat covered his forehead and he really thought he'd throw up all over the priceless manuscript.

He recovered somewhat from his error once he realized no one had seen what he'd done and returned to the book to reread that first bit after the B.

Just as his heart slowed, a wail from the far end of the library broke the silence, startled the guards and caused everyone to stand. Gloria was down on her knees, cell phone dropped to the ground. Dr. Sparks and a guard rushed to her side. Flynn and the other four guests stood at their tables. Flynn first wondered if they would be penalized for standing, as they still had an hour left to spend with the books.

Then he wondered about Gloria.

Selfish.

The guards motioned for the guests to sit. After a few moments of whispered talk with the guard and the German, Dr. Sparks came to the tables to address the five guests. "Ladies and gentlemen, Gloria just received word that her ten-year-old twins were killed in an automobile accident. Out of compassion for her and the staff, we have decided to conclude this evening's event. We will attempt to make this up to you some other way, but for now we need you to step away from the tables and exit the building with the guard."

The two ladies in the group started crying. The other two men were solemn. Flynn stood, staring down at the B and the story he would never finish.

He read the first few sentences again.

We told you to beware. The Woskits are everywhere. Stealing the breath of the young and creating turmoil for the mothers.

Another wail. This one chilled him to the bone.

One of the lady guards slumped against the middle table, nearly landing on the ancient text. The German came running and another guard rushed to her side.

"My son," she choked.

Flynn felt dizzy. Three children. Two mothers.

It couldn't be. He shut the book, afraid to read any more. He pulled the gloves off and stepped away from the table. Great drops of sweat rolled from his forehead.

A burning sensation bloomed on the palm of his hand.

There, where his skin had touched the illumination, was a gold imprint. He tried to wipe it off on his jeans, to no avail. He ran his fingers across the palm of his hand and the gold wouldn't budge.

Dr. Sparks unlocked the door for the weeping ladies. He stood there while the rest of the guests gathered their belongings and their senses and started for the exit.

Flynn stopped by the bathroom with the approval of the stern-faced guard. He looked at himself in the mirror. Pale and sweaty would be an improvement from what he saw. He turned on the faucet and tried to wash the burning gold off his hand. He let the water run over it while he focused on the sign above the sink. *Employees must wash hands before returning to work.*

He pulled his hand out of the water. The gold was still there, and if he looked closely, he could make out the details of the B and the serpents. He turned the handle off on the faucet, but the water kept coming.

He twisted the handle back and forth, but nothing worked.

He must be losing his mind.

The other three sinks slowly started to drip, then trickle, then flowed full force. The soap dispensers were oozing into the basins, mixing with the water and creating an overflowing cascade of bubbles that spilled onto the floor.

Flynn stumbled backward and out the bathroom door, ever so glad to see the guard motioning for him to leave the building.

He reached the door, nodded a weak condolence to Dr. Sparks and the guard, who were donning their jackets, and went out into the crisp night air. He turned back to see Dr. Sparks removing the *Library Closed for Private Event* sign.

And then the door slammed shut with the guard and Dr. Sparks still inside. Flynn thought it might be the wind, but there was no wind.

Dr. Sparks and the guard tried the key again. They tried yanking and tugging on the door. Flynn took the steps two at a time back to the entrance and tried to pull on the door. He saw the lights inside the building go dark, starting at the rear of the hall, then the chandelier over the entrance, and then the wrought iron lamps on either side of the entryway. If Flynn hadn't seen what had happened, he would have thought the library was empty.

"Dr. Sparks, are you all right?"

Nothing. No movement. Not a sound. Pitch black.

He reached into his pocket for his phone, but remembered he'd left it at his apartment as he hadn't wanted to be bothered tonight.

Flynn sank down to the steps to catch his breath and wipe away the sweat that stung his eyes. The pain in his hand increased, and he could see flashes of gold even in the dim moonlight.

He convinced his legs to stand and made his way toward the street hoping to flag down a passerby to call the police. Flynn had no idea whether the people in the library were hurt or even alive.

He glanced in both directions, but traffic was light. He finally heard a vehicle approaching from behind, and turned to see the *No Parking Anytime* street sign. The blue sedan rolled past, but he could see a panicked look on the driver's face and the brake lights flashing on and off frantically. The sedan had a mind of its own and failed to heed to Flynn's frantic waving. He put his hands on his knees and stifled the urge to lie down on the ground and give up. He'd never been strong, and now, well. He didn't know what he was now.

The screech of metal on metal startled him. Four cars previously parked on the opposite side of the street started moving slowly, bumpers scraping against one another. The sedan joined the bumper-to-bumper roll down the street.

Flynn panicked. Then remembered all he'd read this evening…

No parking.

Library closed.

Wash hands.

Mothers' turmoil.

Breath of the young.

Flynn turned and ran toward his apartment, four blocks away. He kept his eyes down as best he could without stumbling into anything. Out of breath after one block, legs and stomach cramping after two blocks, he paused briefly to catch his breath. He took off again at a full sprint and managed to keep his eyes on the sidewalk. A dog barked in the distance, startling him, and he sidestepped into the alley just half a block from home.

He went about fifty feet into the alley between the side entrances of the bakery and the pawn shop. Hands on knees once again, he tried to gather himself and catch his breath. The searing pain in his left hand was almost unbearable.

But he was almost home.

Then, out of the corner of his eye, Flynn O'Hare saw the sign on the pawn shop door. He closed his eyes, but only after his brain had processed the images. A dark wolf, baring fangs and blood-red eyes, and the warning in golden letters:

Trespassers Will Be Shot.

ALONE: A LEGACY TALE

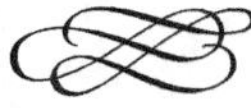

When Sandra falters in her role as caretaker of a magical pair of eyeglasses—and the vintage phone book that pairs with them—a huge void threatens to swallow her. Can Sandra dial the right number for a bit of wisdom from beyond before the loneliness overtakes her?

*S*andra Rose pulled her coat collar tighter around her neck and scaled the steps to Sandusky High. The last day before winter break. The last day of final exams.

And her brain was as empty, and yet as full, as Granny's brittle old telephone book.

Sandra stuffed her coat into her locker and tucked the flyaway staticky blonde strands back into the messy bun on her head. She didn't use the small mirror affixed inside her locker to touch up her makeup. She'd not done that all school year. If the pale concealer and light pink blush had slid from her freckled face on the bus ride here, so be it.

People could take her like she came or not at all.

Most chose not at all.

Sandra had inherited her deceased grandmother's reading glasses last August, along with a 1957 United Telephone Company directory with blank pages. Not one number, not one address, not a single black-and-white advertisement.

Only blank pages.

Blank pages that held the answers to any question one cared to ask —if one donned the golden spectacles with the etched green vines and dancing cobalt butterflies on the frames before viewing the page. Any question.

Well, almost any question.

Dozens of lockers slammed shut, sending ear-crushing metal-on-metal clangs bouncing off the cinderblock walls. Other students walked shoulder to shoulder, heads close, and bumping into each other. Telling of Christmas plans and date nights and teacher gossip. But Sandra spoke to no one.

And no one spoke to her.

Like a mindless amoeba, the mass of bodies divided and disappeared behind various doors along the hallway. Sandra slid into her back-corner desk by the window, the position she coveted in all her classes. She'd not studied for this final. She'd not needed to. Her grade was high enough that she didn't even need to take the final to pass the class.

Ditto for all her classes. She was just going through the motions. Biding her time.

Thanks to the blank pages in Granny's phone book and those cobalt blue butterflies.

Mr. Glowaki slapped a half dozen test packets to each student in the front row, and one by one, the tests were passed to the back of the class. Glowaki sat behind his monstrous oak desk, noted the time, and announced they had thirty minutes to spill five months of British Literature learning onto the pages.

Sandra was tempted to leave the pages as blank as Granny's phone book. Write down a simple ten-digit phone number giving the teacher all the answers he'd ever need and tell Glowaki exactly where he could stuff his test.

She picked up her pencil and tried to shake off the attitude. She knew it wasn't fair. He was doing his job, meaningless as it was, and Sandra just wanted this year to be done. Graduate.

Leave Sandusky.

Leave the well-meaning people around her and start a life somewhere else where her bad attitude and moping wouldn't bring everyone else such concern.

Without a dresser drawer full of memories haunting her every night.

But June was an eternity from now, and for now, Sandra joined the students in front of her, stuck in the adolescent amoeba, as they hunched over their tests, dragging their No. 2's across the sheets, flipping pages, and bobbing nervous legs up and down under the desks. She scribbled a few answers. Shakespeare's meaning by this. Chaucer's intent with this. On and on.

Fifteen minutes in, the window pulled her attention. The sky was two shades grayer than when she'd stepped off the bus. And the flakes were swirling. Not heavy or soaking, more like loose lace bits floating in the wind. Unsure of whether to land or keep floating.

Mindless.

Sandra figured a fifty percent would keep her on the honor roll, so she stopped answering the questions at about the half-way mark. She put the tip of her pencil on the paper and began to doodle in the margins, mindless. Floating pencil strokes as light as the snowflakes and as gray as the sky. Loose and lacy. Not really seeing. Just coping.

Hoping.

Wishing.

Disconnecting.

She had moments of disconnect when Granny was still around. Always just slightly an outsider. Despite hosting slumber parties. Despite keeping her nose clean. Despite this and that…

But these moments of time-freezes were this year. Worse since she'd slid those spectacles onto her own face and started flipping pages and dialing numbers.

And she missed Elizabeth Rose Galloway with a fiery passion. Granny.

Thanksgiving without Granny was awful.

Soon the first Christmas without her.

Sandra's upcoming January birthday. Without her.

Where was life's fast-forward button? Skip all the triggers, pretty please.

Mom said Sandra simply had a bad case of the "bad attitudes." Or maybe it was grief. Or both. And by the way, would you like to see a therapist?

Sandra declined.

Dad said she just hadn't found her "group" yet, though by one's senior year, the group Sandra belonged to should have emerged by now—if it even existed.

It didn't.

Despite MVP on the volleyball team. Despite attending junior prom with a not-too-geeky guy on her shoulder. Despite her best efforts at socialization, Granny had been her "group."

Finding one now would be futile. Sandra, upright and functioning, though barely, felt mostly lopsided in her approach to everything.

Glowaki called time up, pulling Sandra from her trance. Everyone shuffled and some moaned and raised their arms to stretch. A couple of kids exhaled, likely having held their breath for the last forty minutes as their graduation status rode on their exam grade.

Sandra looked down at her paper.

Graphite vines, twisting and leafy, spread up the margins of the test. Butterflies in stunning monotone gray detail darted between the leaves. Almost moving. Almost real.

Shimmering silver flecks of depth.

And green sparks of glitter all around the edges.

Sandra shook her head and rubbed her eyes. She flipped the test packet closed, hiding the pulsating artwork under the answered pages, and cursed under her breath.

She should've left the dumb thing blank.

She should've fought off the urge to float out of her head toward the dancing crystals outside.

The pull of Granny's readers and the blank phone book pages waiting for her back home was overwhelming. All consuming. All those blank pages just waiting to be explored.

Filling her mind up one moment.

Erasing everything the next.

Blank.

The only thing that wasn't blank in Sandra's life was Granny's handwritten note.

Written well before the old woman passed.

Accompanying the mysterious reading glasses.

Delivered by a pudgy man in a sweaty suit that humid August night of Elizabeth Rose Gallaway's funeral.

MOM AND DAD would be home soon. Sandra spread across her bed and let the day's stress seep from her muscles into the mattress. Sleep rarely came easy before Granny died. Nights were filled with phone books and green sparks. A nap now was out of the question since her parents would barge in with the tree soon.

But the thought of drifting off into a parallel existence was tantalizing…

She reached for her nightstand drawer and pulled out the glasses case and the phone book. She toyed with the edges of the pages, letting them fan gently to the back cover. She kept the glasses in their case, but rested one hand on them, feeling the warm hum they gave.

Her family thought her to be wallowing in dangerous grief—and to an extent she was—sitting here in her room for hours on end. Playing with glasses and Granny Google's phone book. Sandra should be getting past this. Past the grief. Past the holding onto strange mementos.

Everyone had thought Granny to have a photographic memory. That the old woman had in all her spare time memorized every telephone number in the states. Ask the old gal anything. She'd slide on her glasses, grin sideways, and pull out the old phone book.

With the blank pages.

Scan the page with a well-worn, arthritic finger, grin again, then rattle off a phone number.

Ten digits. The one who asked the question would call the number to be greeted with a voice on the other end in the specialty of the realm of the question.

What's the best recipe for peanut brittle? A confectioner in California had that answer. And was willing to share their family's process.

A neighbor out in the country asked how to keep his horse from pacing. Granny came up with the number for an equine behavioralist. In Kentucky. With the answer. From a Philadelphia phone directory.

On and on. Sandra had asked many questions of Granny. From 4-H projects to volleyball moves to family dynamics. Most ended with a number and a telephone call.

The family stuff. Granny didn't need to "look somethin' up right quick" for any of those. She just knew. How to stifle the strife. How to navigate raging emotions. How to be, well… How to be Sandra's best friend.

Sandra sat up straight, cross-legged on the bed, pulled the glasses from their resting place, and slid them onto her face. The chain dangled from the readers on either side of her cheeks. The room went blurry. Everything but the dead center of the phone book cover. That view was crystal clear.

Sandra thought for a moment. Over the last few months, she'd asked of the book—or maybe she was asking the glasses, she wasn't sure where the phenomenon originated—all manner of questions. It started simply enough.

That night of the funeral.

With the delivery from the sweaty man and the note from Granny. She'd called Sandra her Legacy in the note she'd left.

Sandra didn't feel very legacy-worthy, and her behavior toward her family once school started proved it.

Her abuse of the phone book's powers sealed the verdict.

Unworthy.

She'd used the book to get answers to test questions. Thus the honor roll status—a feat she was well able on her own to accomplish, but why put forth the effort when the crutch is right there in her nightstand?

And the more she asked of it, abused it, the greater the pull.

Sandra was addicted.

Granny never showed signs of that. Addiction. As far as Sandra knew, her grandmother would go days or weeks or months even without putting on the glasses and reading off phone numbers.

But Sandra wanted more. *Needed* more. She wanted to understand. She begged the book and the glasses and the blue butterflies for a sign. Over and over. What to do next. No answer. Should she leave her family early? Before graduation? Why Sandra? Why not just let her be in her grief and be normal? No answer.

What was on this semester's chem test?

Well, those blue butterflies had floated to life, vines springing up in all directions, carrying a three-dimensional rendering of a ten-digit phone number.

That Sandra called.

And the voice on the other end? A previous student, Craig-something, had saved his notes and would send them to Sandra. Free of charge.

And not just notes arrived the next week. But a copy of the test. And a "let's keep in touch" hand-scribbled note from the young man. She looked him up on Facebook. Nice looking kid. Dark hair. Blue eyes. A couple of years older than Sandra. She pecked out the beginnings of a private message to the kid.

But when the green sparks began dancing around the screen, she'd slammed the laptop shut and that was that.

Sandra didn't keep in touch. Never even sent the poor guy a thank you. She just took.

Consumed.

Used up.

Sandra sighed and pulled her attention back to the present as she heard car doors slamming outside. Her parents were home.

Quickly, she rattled off a question. "Will I survive this Christmas?"

She opened the book.

Nothing.

No vines. No wings. No buds. Not even the first green spark.

"What's the best sugar cookie recipe?"

That? *That* stupid request got her a phone number. She dialed it on her cell. "The Great Cake Bakery, how may I help you?" Sandra didn't ask what state. She didn't ask of the lady about sugar cookies, cakes, or pies.

Sandra hung up. She didn't need to know any more recipes or project instructions. She didn't want or need any more test help.

Sandra wanted peace. And answers.

The glasses went back in their case; Sandra carefully slid the lenses in first, allowing the chain to snake in behind. The book and glasses went back to the nightstand drawer.

She threw some words toward the ceiling, hoping they'd make their way past the plaster and rafters and shingles. All the way to wherever Granny may be. "Why me? Why did you ever leave me those stupid spectacles?"

Sandra paused on the way out of her bedroom. She could hear her parents fussing over the tree. How to set it up. No, not this way. That way. No, not that side front. The other side is fuller.

Then she asked, "Why did you leave me here alone?"

~

SANDRA SETTLED the score between Mom and Dad, splitting the difference of the arguments. Give Mom a win. Give Dad a win. In the end, they were content, and the tree was upright—albeit lopsided. The branches drooped with balls and bells. Sandra watered the base and covered the stand with their quilted tree skirt—one that Granny had sewn by hand.

As her parents retreated to the kitchen to argue over dinner preparations, a green sparkle caught Sandra's eye. At first she dismissed it. She pinched her arm. Those sparks came when she was dissociating, like during the exam, or when the phone book was working its magic.

More sparks.

Another pinch to be sure she was in the moment.

She stepped closer to the branches, still slightly cool with a faint wisp of true outdoorsy pine. She pulled a couple of branches to the side, on the "bad side" as Mom had called it and peered inside. Near the base of the trunk, twisting vines had begun to sprout. She pulled the tree skirt back and looked in the water basin. Still full. Nothing unusual. The vines started a few inches above the stand's rim.

She put the skirt back and continued the examination. Blue chrysalises with gold seams dangled from the inner branches. Tiny. Smaller than kidney beans.

"Hey, Dad? Did they shake this tree?" Sandra had gone with her parents in years past to the Christmas tree farm. The best part of the whole experience was watching the workers place the tree in a mechanical "shaker." At first she thought it was to rid their purchase of loose pine needles. But she'd seen enough mice, squirrels, and birds flee from the branches of their fallen homes to know loose pine needles were just a bonus.

"Shook it till it cried uncle." Sandra rolled her eyes. Dad jokes. "Why?" He came around the corner, drying his hands on a dish towel.

"Do you see those? They look like chrysalis." She pointed toward the trunk, past the white lights and garland.

He leaned in. Even tipped his glasses over his eyebrows to peer naked eyed into the tree. "Nope. Don't see a thing." He patted her on the shoulder. "No worries. Nothing could've hung on but the branches after the shaking the tree elves gave this beauty." He straightened the star on the top and went back to the kitchen.

Sandra leaned in. Chrysalises. Dotted with glowing cobalt. Lined with silken blue. Shimmering. Shaking just the slightest.

The clearer the edges of the wraps became, and the wings more visible, the longer she stared through the branches. The veins. The antennae.

Then more green sparkles—and not from the tree branches swaying in the furnace vent against the clear twinkle lights.

One chrysalis shook violently, the cobalt seam splitting down the middle. Out tumbled a butterfly no bigger than a quarter, upside down and pumping its wings as if inhaling and exhaling with every motion.

It righted itself, pumped its wings once more, the green sparkles emanating from the tips, then flew toward Sandra's face then up the staircase. Startled, she toppled backward and landed in the doorway to the kitchen as a dozen other butterflies emerged from the Christmas tree, taking a winged migration upward.

Her parents turned from food prep to see what the thud was. Dad stood over her, taco tray at the ready, meat steaming and shredded cheese falling off the edge and into Sandra's hair. "If I'd known you were this famished, we'd have cooked before we put up the tree."

BACK IN HER ROOM, tree properly trimmed and stomach full of obligatory taco dinner, Sandra found a hoard of butterflies, wings bobbing, antennae swaying. On her bedspread. On her nightstand. Her lamp. The volleyball trophies.

She was careful as she stepped onto the rug for fear of crushing one under her socked feet. She closed her door. Gently. So her parents wouldn't rush to her grieving aid.

Sandra made her way to the bed, the noiseless fluttering of the wings pounded in her head, green glittery sparks sprayed outward with every flit and turn of their antennae. The pull toward the glasses and phonebook were like no other she'd felt in all these months. Deep breaths and rubbing her temples didn't relieve the suffocating pressure.

She pulled open the dresser drawer, sending a few of the insects scurrying for the bed posts. She fumbled the glasses out of their case, her fingers tangling in the chain, and put them on. She slid the phonebook onto her bed and sat, hoping whatever was under her path downward to the bedspread had enough sense to move before she could no longer stand.

She tried to clear her head to ask the most pertinent question of the book. The one that would likely bring a viable number instead of a blank, blurry page.

"Where did all of these butterflies come from?"

Green sparks oozed from the edges of the book. The vines twisted and turned upward, but the butterflies, her cobalt companions from the months past, had turned brown and gray. As gray as the graphite doodle on her exam paper. As the vines twisted out into three-dimension those butterflies fell away, crumbling to ash around her hands and lap. On the book page.

Smearing on her white bedspread like someone had emptied a pencil sharpener.

Panic set in. Breathing hurt. Searing headache nearly forced her eyelids shut. "Please, Granny. I don't know what to do."

She felt a brush against her cheek. Then another. The newly hatched butterflies brushed against her face. Her hair. Her wrists. They came from the bedpost, the lamp, the dresser. Floor. Trophies.

They gathered on the now-dingy phonebook page.

Then they merged with the vines, wings pumping, spraying green bits of glitter.

Then the number appeared. Shimmering, translucent ten-digit number. Sandra grabbed for her cell phone and tapped in the number.

"Sandra Rose?"

Her heart skipped at the gravelly voice. The same one that had greeted her after the funeral last summer when she'd first experienced the magic of the glasses. The same one that had been her single-woman tribe for most of Sandra's life. Elizabeth Rose Gallaway.

That number, from last summer, she'd tried to dial over and over again. Sometimes dozens of times a day. But it had only worked that once. And it had only been for a few seconds. "Carry on my Legacy." And I love you. And be good. That was all Granny had had time to say then before the line went dead.

No instructions.

No reasons why.

No warnings.

And now she heard her grandmother's voice again. From a new number. Brought by a new batch of butterflies.

"Granny?" Sandra managed a broken word, barely audible over the ringing in her ears. Tears stung hot down her cheeks.

"Sandra. You've been burning through the pages pretty heavy, huh?"

"Yes." Like a child caught with her hand in the cookie jar before dinner.

"Have you learned anything?"

She straightened on the bed. "It's addictive. I can't get enough. I'm all alone. I don't understand why…"

"Enough with the 'I's', child. This gift isn't about you. Continue to use the magic for self-gain, and this batch of Christmas butterflies will go the way of the others."

"I miss you."

"Oh, my darling. It's the first Christmas without me. I remember the first holidays without loved ones. It's hard. But you're stronger than you know. These new winged ones are the last gift I can give you. Take care of them."

Sandra reached with her free hand for the vines and the floating number. The butterflies, now imperceptible to touch, toyed with her fingertips. The number faded. The vines retracted as the insects lighted on various leaves.

A fresh wave of panic washed over her as she sensed the conversation was about to end.

"But I'm still alone."

"No dear, Sandra. You're not. Answer the doorbell."

Then Granny Google was gone. Disconnected.

The greenery and butterflies and emerald sparks all sucked back into the blank pages of the vintage phone directory.

Not even the dust from the batch of cobalts Sandra had killed remained.

All of it gone.

Sandra dried her cheeks and put away her Granny's items back into the drawer as the doorbell rang.

Sandra wasn't even surprised to hear it. She headed down the steps to answer it before her parents could. She figured Granny had sent the fat, sweaty man in the suit, the ornery old woman's version of a Santa Claus, to deliver her another package. Maybe this one had some instructions and the warning label or something.

She swung the front door open. The first thing she saw were green sparks dancing around a brown paper package tied with a cobalt blue ribbon in gloved hands.

The next thing Sandra Rose saw was Craig-something-or-other, the owner of those gloved hands and the chemistry notes smiling at her. Black curls peeking from under a beanie. Kind blue eyes. A bit of emerald around the edges.

"I, uh. I got a message." He held the box out for her to take. She did.

She was barely able to keep upright—lopsided, actually—against the doorframe, turning the small box over and over in her hands, staring into those blue eyes.

"Well, silly, aren't you going to invite him in?"

She looked over her shoulder to see her parents standing, grinning like buffoons next to the tree, upright but lopsided.

Sandra stepped aside and Craig made his way inside to introduce himself. The package hummed in her hands. She longed to scale the steps, rip open the paper, and…

She stopped. Thought. About the dust of cobalt insects and the mess she'd made of the last few months. She watched as the three others in the room laughed and made small talk. Dad offered him a taco and a couple of bad jokes.

Sandra shut the door to the cold and knelt down at the tree. The skirt Granny had sewn. She placed the package—unopened—on the skirt.

And she joined in. Stayed downstairs. Open. Engaged.

Not alone.

THE CAMERA

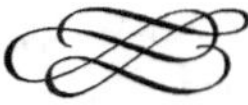

For Marshall, a small-time movie studio chief, the stress of his job is overwhelming as he nears his latest deadline. When he receives an idol in the mail that claims to predict the success of any film project ahead of time, he must tread carefully to heed all of the instructions, lest he makes a terrible mistake...

*S*ome things happen fast, as one would expect. A car speeding down the road, spinning an empty Walmart sack into the air, or sending discarded pop cans clanking across the pavement.

Or a dog bite. Dog bites happen quickly.

Even things that take a long time can happen fast. One minute, a nurse in pink scrubs hands over a wriggling, wailing five-pound sack of flour to love and care for. The next minute, five years later, that flour sack walks into kindergarten, and it may or may not turn back to blow a kiss. Five years after that, in two blinks, two more flour sacks require food, shelter and love.

Marshall straightened his tie and shook his head. Nostalgia wasn't his style, so he wasn't sure where it had come from. The only feeling he held hands with lately was exhaustion. He drove his editors nuts, prompting them to get his latest film completely spliced, timed to the score and credited, completely perfect and ready for the test screenings with the all-star cast and a few hundred of their closest friends. He couldn't fail. Not this time.

He whipped off the tie and unbuttoned the top two buttons of his blue collared shirt. Not today. He didn't have the patience to be put together today.

Downstairs, Tammy wrangled the kids around the table. Eggs in the baby's hair. Eggs on the floor. Eggs in the Shih Tzu's prissy black coat, the dog twirling and twisting trying to eat the scraps from its own back.

"You joining us?"

"No." Marshall grabbed two pieces of dry toast and his thermos of coffee Tammy had ready for him. There was no time today. "I'll see you later." He kissed each of them and turned for a second, taking in the scene.

Three flour sacks, a wife and a wheelbarrow's worth of bills that would go unpaid if *The Café* flopped at the box office.

It had certainly happened fast.

Marshall pulled the front door shut behind him, then nearly

tripped down the front steps over a box sitting on the butterfly welcome mat. His name stood out in red letters on the label, with no postage or return address. He tucked it under his arm, wondered briefly who'd left it for him before he tossed it in the passenger's seat. He crammed both pieces of toast into his mouth and drove to the studio.

～

"Mr. Osgood, there's a problem with the music piece. Freddie says it's copyrighted, but we had the original score—"

Marshall snatched the file from the secretary's hand. "I'll look into it."

He opened the folder and three more people stood in his doorway, all with problems, all delivering stress to him in neat and tidy eight-by-eleven manila envelopes.

"Get everyone in the foyer. Now!" They jumped and left him alone. The small corner studio wasn't big-time, but it had produced some hits. The staff was talented. Some of them Marshall had hand-picked just for this project.

But everything was falling flat. One more setback and the over-time would kill the budget.

Marshall massaged the back of his neck and downed the rest of the coffee from the thermos. He joined his team in the foyer. Some of them stood cross-armed, others stared at their feet.

He exploded on them. He wanted no more excuses. No more missed deadlines. Make it work. They had too much at stake.

When he realized two of the ladies were stifling sobs, he lowered his voice and softened his tone.

"Look, we're in the home stretch. It's almost ready to come together. Let's see the fruit of this thing. *Café* is gonna be great, we just need to get it done." He shooed them back to their posts.

He took the secretary by her arm before she could leave. "I'm going out for a drive. I've gotta get calmed down."

"Sure, Mr. Osgood. I'll forward your messages?"

"No, just post them on my door. I won't be gone long."

He sat in his car in the dimly lit parking garage until he could no longer feel the heartbeat in his throat. A few deep breaths, and he headed for the drive-through deli on Lexington and over to Cramer Park. He rolled down all the windows and let the humidity-free breeze blow off the residual anger.

This morning he'd thought about the passing of time and how things happen fast. Today, at the studio, nothing happened fast. Everything was going in slow-motion and he felt every second all the way to his bones.

He decided to check out the box from the porch. The white label with his name in red sat on the top. The rest of the ten-by-ten-inch box was black with green trim, much like those poison control stickers Tammy plastered all over everything so the kids would know not to drink the drain cleaner.

He took a huge bite of his pastrami and popped the lid off the box to reveal an old-time movie camera model nestled in tissue paper. He wiped his hands on his pants and carefully removed the recorder. Two reels sat on the top for the film—like Mickey Mouse ears, his daughter had said when she'd seen the antique camera the studio used for lobby décor. He turned the tiny handle, and the reels and minuscule film moved in response. The detail was impeccable.

He sat the camera in the seat and looked over the box. No return address. No sender indicated. A very cool piece. Maybe his wife had left it for him. She knew the stress he was under. But she shouldn't have spent the money.

He pulled out the white tissue paper and tossed it on the back floorboard along with half of his sandwich. A lined index card was taped in the bottom. He pulled it out and held it at arm's length to read. Bifocals had to be on the to-do list soon.

Someone had taken the time to write a gag. It had to be. In lime green ink the "directions" read:

Ask the Camera about your next project and "Roll Film." If you have a masterpiece idea, or an impending disaster, the Camera will let you know. Use with caution.

He picked up the camera and tried to find the "Made in China" sticker, but didn't see one. He shook his head and then considered playing along.

He looked around the park. A grown man talking to a motion picture camera figurine in his car probably wouldn't fare too well with passerby mothers. When he was satisfied no one was paying attention to him, he said, "What's for dinner?" and turned the crank.

Nothing happened.

"Well, will Tammy's dinner be a masterpiece or a disaster?" Another turn of the handle, and still nothing happened.

One more time. This time he decided to follow the directions and actually ask about a project—his pet project for the past three years. "Will *The Café* be a masterpiece or a disaster?"

He turned the crank.

The reels turned and the film cycled around each, disappearing into the camera.

The piece buzzed in his hand like his beard trimmers. He nearly threw the thing on the floorboard, but recovered before he dropped it. A one-by-two-inch piece of black paper ejected from the back of the camera. He carefully pulled it, and it fell into his hand. It looked like film, black with tiny perforations along the top and bottom edges. As he held it in his palm, red lettering glistened in the middle.

Disaster.

He put the camera back in its box and threw the paper on the floor. Then he burst out laughing, which got the attention of a couple of overweight joggers through the open windows. He recovered and massaged his brows.

The stress of the project, the blow-up at the office, and the weight of family turmoil. And here he was, a grown man losing it, talking to a novelty gag gift and nearly wetting his pants in the process.

He reached for the paper. It wasn't the same size as the tiny film strips attached to the reels. He examined the camera, but couldn't find a place to reload the strips. He'd love to share this around the office, but if he couldn't refill it, he'd just keep it for himself.

His cell phone vibrated in his pocket. A quick check revealed five missed calls in the last hour.

Time to stop playing games and face the music.

~

HE SHOWED the camera to Tammy that evening, and she denied leaving it. He tried to demonstrate it for her, but it wouldn't work. When he showed her the little black notecard, she denied being able to see the "Disaster" printed in red.

He chided her for teasing him, but Lydia, the first-grader, couldn't see it either. They were all in on it.

The rest of the day at the studio had gone poorly. One disaster after another. *The Café* was firmly in the red.

After everyone had gone to bed, Marshall sat on the couch with the camera. He ran his finger over the reels and the slot where the paper came out. Then he whispered, "Will *The Café* be a masterpiece or a disaster?" He turned the handle.

The camera hummed and the reels spun. Out popped a black card. *Asked and Answered.*

His eyes widened, and he set the camera on the couch and took the stairs two at a time. He woke Tammy up and shoved the card in her face. "See it? Can you read this one?"

"Marshall, it's late." She rubbed her eyes and tried to focus on the card. "See what? It's the same black card you showed us earlier. There's no writing on it." She flopped to the pillow.

He couldn't believe it. He stomped downstairs.

He spent the rest of the night asking about *The Café* and turning the handle. At least fifty black cards, all with variations of *Disaster, Give It Up,* and *Asked and Answered.*

It had to be getting low on paper. Not too much more could fit in the back compartment, which he also tried to pry open, to no avail.

He heard his alarm clock go off from the upstairs bedroom and realized daylight was peeking through the curtains.

When Tammy saw him sitting in the middle of the floor, little black cards all around him, she shook her head with that look of disappointment when he would tell her he had to work late. She went to the kitchen, where she banged pots and pans much louder than was necessary.

He realized what a pathetic mess he must seem to her. He rose and brushed the cards off his lap. He showered, shaved and downed four ibuprofens before heading to the kitchen. He sat at the table as the kids trickled down the stairs one at a time.

"Tammy. *Café's* gonna fail."

She stopped stirring the pancake batter and looked him square in the eyes. "Because the camera told you so, or because it was gonna fail anyway?"

"Both. Anyway. I don't know. I just know it's not going to work and we're going to be in trouble."

She poured the batter on the griddle with a sizzle. He helped situate the girls and passed out their plates.

"Well, maybe you should cancel it before it sucks any more money out of the studio."

"Maybe." He glanced toward the couch and the camera laughed back at him.

"And not because the camera said so." She pointed the dripping spatula at him. "Because you're a responsible man and you know when to cut your losses."

He kissed her on the cheek, ate breakfast with his kids, snuck the camera into his briefcase, then went to the studio to lay off the crew.

THE OFFICE WAS EMPTY. Hollowness reigned where hustle and bustle had filled the place just hours before. He'd cut everyone their last checks and sent them home.

He sat alone at his desk and pulled the green and black box from his case. He'd been careful before he'd left not to let Tammy see him take the camera. "Will *The Café* be a masterpiece or a disaster?"

The black card told him he *"Made the Right Decision."*

He sat back in the chair and stared at the device. He had to be imagining things.

He pulled a file from the bottom pile on his desk—his "Great Idea" folder in which he'd write down bits and pieces of plot, storyline and characters. Several ideas were simply titles with no story attached yet.

One after the other, he asked the camera about his ideas. Each time, the camera buzzed, spun and gave him a black card with red lettering.

Every idea was a disaster.

He paced back and forth, asking and turning, brainstorming.

Every time, the camera spat out a negative card.

He dug out the index card with the handwritten directions. He'd followed the directions. All except the "use with caution" part. He'd asked the camera questions with reckless abandon for a day now.

Then it struck him.

He'd just laid off dozens of people and canceled a production that was nearly finished based on a few rough days and the advice of a gizmo.

One more question. One more try. "Would a movie about a stressed-out schmuck that listens to a fortune-telling camera and ruins his life be a masterpiece or a disaster?" He slowly turned the handle. The camera vibrated. Out popped a card with green lettering.

Blockbuster!

ABOUT THE AUTHOR

Beth enjoys chucking words into sentences then standing back to see what magic—or mayhem—falls out, crafting tales in mystery, sci-fi, fantasy, and general "slice of life" fiction. She couldn't accomplish this without the help of her tutu-clad Little Miss Muse and Trudi the Concrete Office Goose, who's partial to superhero capes.

Her stories have appeared in multiple publications, including Pulphouse Fiction Magazine and Ellery Queen Mystery Magazine, and in multiple fiction anthologies. She's received several Honorable Mentions from Writers of the Future. Her lighthearted blog peeks into the writing life as she pokes fun at herself and her circus of a life.

Follow the antics of Little Miss Muse and Trudi, read Beth's blog (she might have burned down her kitchen last week), and discover the stories at bapaul.com.

ALSO BY B. A. PAUL

Short Story Collections

Spunk and Spice, Volumes 1 and 2: A Collection of six short stories celebrating timeless wit and wisdom.

Out There, Volumes 1 and 2: A Collection of six short sci-fi and speculative tales.

Mystery Minutes, Volumes 1 and 2: Six short mystery stories

All the Feels, Volumes 1, 2, and 3: Collections of inspiring short stories

Just a Tick of Whimsy, Volumes 1 and 2: Collections of fantasy shorts.

Hijacked Holidays: Definitely not your warm-and-fuzzy winter tales.

Dark Minds: Toe-curling twisted mysteries.

Blog Compilations: Slices of the writing life with lots of laughs and bumps in the road.

Life Along the Way

Life All Over Again

Novels

Triage

Young Adult (or Young at Heart) Books

Switch: Book 1 in the Oliver Andrews Trilogy

STAY IN TOUCH!

BAPAUL.COM

Take a glimpse into B.A. Paul's writing journey, including the ups and downs of managing family, "real jobs," ducks in wobbling rows, and chasing down her Little Miss Muse. New blog posts go up Mondays, with the first Monday of the Month reserved for a free fiction short story available on the blog for a limited time.

Newsletter Signup!
Click here to sign up for the newsletter and receive a free exclusive short story!
Get the latest release information, author updates, and exclusive content.